Henry P. Stephens, Edward Solomon

Billie Taylor

Or, the Reward of Vvirtue

Henry P. Stephens, Edward Solomon

Billie Taylor
Or, the Reward of Vvirtue

ISBN/EAN: 9783743419681

Manufactured in Europe, USA, Canada, Australia, Japa

Cover: Foto ©Andreas Hilbeck / pixelio.de

Manufactured and distributed by brebook publishing software (www.brebook.com)

Henry P. Stephens, Edward Solomon

Billie Taylor

.

Original Nautical Comic Opera.

Billee Taylor.

BY
STEPHENS & SOLOMON

BOSTON:

OLIVER DITSON & COMPANY.

New York: C. H. DITSON & CO. Chicago: LYON & HEALY. Philadelphia: J. E. DITSON

Nautical Comic Opera
in two acts.

BILLEE TAYLOR;

OR,

"THE REWARD OF VIRTUE,"

BY

Henry P. Stephens,

AND

EDWARD SOLOMON.

———•+•———

BOSTON:

Oliver Ditson & Co.

DITSON & CO.,	LYON & HEALY,	J. E. DITSON & CO.,
New York.	Chicago.	Philadelphia.

DRAMATIS PERSONÆ.

CAPTAN THE HON. FELIX FLAPPER, R. N.,
of H.M.S. "Thunderbomb" . . . . *2d Tenor.*
SIR MINCING LANE, Knight . . . . *2d Tenor.*
BILLEE TAYLOR. . . . *Tenor.*
BEN BARNACLE . . . . *Baritone.*
CHRISTOPHER CRAB. . . . *Baritone.*

PHŒBE FAIRLEIGH . . . . *Soprano*
ARABELLA LANE . . . . . *Contralto*
ELIZA DABSEY . . . . . .
SUSAN . . . .
JANE SCRAGGS . . . . . .

CHARITY GIRLS.

ARGUMENT.

THE story of this opera is founded on the old song of "Billy Taylor," a well-known English nautical ditty.

The time of the action in 1805, when the press-gang was in full sway. .

The First Act opens with a view of Southampton harbor, at the old inn of the Royal George, when the villagers meet to rejoice over the approaching wedding of *Billee Taylor* and *Phœbe*, a charity girl. There is, also, an heiress, *Arabella Lane*, who is in love with *Billee*. She offers him her hand and fortunes, which he refuses. Her father, *Sir Mincing Lane*, a kindhearted old gentleman is going to give the villagers a feast at *Billee's* wedding. He invites his friend, *Captain Flapper*, to join in the festivities. The *Captain* falls in love with *Phœbe* at first sight, and vows that she shall not marry *Billee*. A tutor, *Crab*, is also in love with *Phœbe*. Among *Captain Flapper's* crew is *Ben Barnacle*, who has gone to sea on account of his love for *Eliza*, who has forsaken him for another lover. He is ordered by the press-gang to go and carry off *Billee Taylor*. During the festivities preceding the wedding, this plan is executed, and *Billee* is taken away, which brings the first act to a close.

The Second Act (two years having elapsed), opens with its scene laid in Portsmouth harbor. Ships are coming and going, while the sailors and their sweethearts, sit around the docks, watching some sailors dancing a hornpipe. All of the charity girls, among whom is *Phœbe*, have followed *Billee* to sea, disguised as sailor boys. *Billee*, in the meantime, has risen to be a lieutenant. *Sir Mincing Lane*, who has become a commander in the volunteers, appears, and endeavors to induce some of the volunteers to join his company. *Phœbe* is about to enlist, when *Barnacle* interferes, and there is a quarrel between the soldiers and the sailors. *Captain Flapper* stops the fight. Some one tells *Phœbe* that *Billee* has lost his love for her, and loves *Arabella*. She fires a pistol at *Billee* and *Arabella*, whom she sees in company, and is ordered to be shot. She then makes herself known. Matters are finally explained and set right, and all ends happily.

INDEX.

J. FRANK GILES, Music Printer, Boston.

OVERTURE.

Libretto by H. P. STEPHENS.

Music by ED. SOLOMON.

TEMPO DI MARCIA.

4

Allegretto Moderato.

8

ACT I.
TO-DAY, TO-DAY.

No. 1. CHORUS OF PEASANTS. (S. S. T. B.)

SCENE.— *The village green of the village of Southampton. Water. Peasants discoverd.*

10

CHORUS.

three times three, Of Phœ - be fair, and bold Bil - lee, To each good wish - es bring - ing, To

three times three, Of Phœ - be fair, and bold Bil - lee, To each good wish - es bring - ing, To

three times three, Of Phœ - be fair, and bold Bil - lee, To each good wish - es bring - ing, To

each good wish - es bring - ing. Here's to man and wife,....

each good wish - es bring - ing. Here's to man and wife,....

each good wish - es bring - ing. Here's to man and wife,....

12

when the marriage knot is tied, Here's hap - pi - ness, good luck, long life, To the bridegroom and the

when the marriage knot is tied, Here's hap - pi - ness, good luck, long life, To the bridegroom and the

when the marriage knot is tied, Here's hap - pi - ness, good luck, long life, To the bridegroom and the

bride, To the bridegroom, to the bridegroom and the bride. To -

bride, To the bridegroom, to the bridegroom and the bride. To -

bride, And the bride, to the bride - - groom and the bride. To -

Phœ - be fair, and bold Bil - lee, To each good wish - - es, to each good wish-es bringing.

Phœ - be fair, and bold Bil - lee, To each good wish - - es, to each good wish-es bringing.

Phœ - be fair, and bold Bil - lee, To each good wish - - es, to each good wish-es bringing.

(enter Crab.)   CRAB.

What means this

re - vel - ry I pray! What means this re - vel - ry I pray!

f CHORUS.

To-day, to-day is ho-li-day, We'll keep it in the us-ual way.

To-day, to-day is ho-li-day, We'll keep it in the us-ual way.

To-day, to-day is ho-li-day, We'll keep it in the us-ual way.

CRAB.
Moderato.

Yes, as you say, in the us-ual way.

Moderato.

When the vil-lag-er has a ho-li-day, He keeps it in the

16

drink is his de - light; He's the pride of the pub - lic hou - ses. When

drink is his de - light; He's the pride of the pub - lic hou - ses.

drink is his de - light; He's the pride of the pub - lic hou - ses.

drink is his de - light; He's the pride of the pub - lic hou - ses.

filled with ale and beer, Then he knows no fear, And the

18

CHORUS.

Ha, ha, ha, ha, ha, ha, ha,   Ha, ha, ha, ha, ha, ha, ha,   To-

Ha, ha, ha, ha, ha, ha, ha,   Ha, ha, ha, ha, ha, ha, ha,   To-

Ha, ha, ha, ha, ha, ha, ha, ha,   To-

Tempo Io.

cres.

-day, to-day is ho-li-day, We'll keep it in the us-ual way, While wed-ding bells are

-day, to-day is ho-li-day, We'll keep it in the us-ual way, While wed-ding bells are

-day, to-day is ho-li-day, We'll keep, we'll keep it in the us-ual way,

ring - ing, While wed - ding bells are ring - ing, We'll drink the health, with three times three, Of

ring - ing, While wed - ding bells are ring - ing, We'll drink the health, with three times three, Of

While wed - ding bells are ring - ing, We'll drink the health, with three times three, Of

Phœ - be fair, and bold Bil - lee, To each good wish - - es, To each good wish-es bringing, To-

Phœ - be fair, and bold Bil - lee, To each good wish - - es, To each good wish-es bringing, To-

Phœ - be fair, and bold Bil - lee, To each good wish - - es, To each good wish-es bringing, To-

-day, to-day is ho-li-day, To-day, to-day is ho-li-day, To-day, to-

-day, to-day is ho-li-day, To-day, to-day is ho-li-day, To-day, to-

-day, to-day is ho-li-day, To-day, to-day is ho-li-day, To-day, to-

-day is ho - - li - - day!.................

-day is ho - - li - - day!... ....

-day is ho-li-day, is ho-li - day!.................

(exeunt.)

CRAB. The desponding villain—How to prevent the marriage—ELIZA DALSEY—Why she is still a widow—CRAB's declaration of love for PHŒBE frightens ELIZA.. First appearance of the virtuous gardener, WILLIAM TAYLOR. | His self-depreciation—His merits recognized by his old schoolmaster, "Spare the rod and spoil the child"—CRAB is off to his duty. The value of friendship—The pleasures of moral gardening described in the song.

THE VIRTUOUS GARDENER.

No. 2. BALLAD.   Billee Taylor.

1. Let oth - ers prate of grand es - tate, I en - vy not such sta - tion; With hoe and spade, tho' un - der - paid, I fol - low my vo - ca - tion. I would not be a mil - lionaire, A bish - op, ba - ro - net, or lord, For

2. The seeds I sow are sure to grow, The trees I plant all flour - ish; And near and far, my pot-herbs are Well known sick folks to nour - ish. I deft - ly turn the new mown hay, Or neat - ly trim the fair green sward; I

wealth and rank I do not care, Since vir-tue, since vir-tue is its own re-ward. With my
work for eight-teen-pence a day, Since vir-tue, since vir-tue is its own re-ward. With, &c.

ro-ses, and my li-lies, and ge-ra-ni-ums; My ap-ples and my cherries, and my currants, and my plums; My po-

-ta-toes and my turnips, and my fine bro-co-li: Who such a vir-tu-ous gard'ner as I......

Who such a vir-tu-ous gard-'ner as I?

The fatal passion of Miss ARABELLA LANE for her father's retainer—Urged by the nearness of the hour when he will be wedded to another, she endeavors to awaken a spark of interest for herself in WILLIAM's heart, and finally throwing aside all maidenly reserve, joins in

"IFS AND ANDS."

No. 3. DUETT.   Arabella and Billee. (M. S. and T.)

ARABELLA. 1. If you were a mai-den,
BILLEE. 2. If you were a lov-er,

and I was a youth,   My voice, with love, la-den   should whis-per all the truth;   How
and I dam-sel fair,   Quick-ly you'd dis-cov-er   that I'd no love to spare;

appassionato.   *cres.* *ritard.*

I loved you with passion,   how you were my joy,   If you were a maiden,   and I was a boy.
If my troth were plighted,   pray'rs you'd vain employ,   If I were a maiden,   and you were a boy.

CHORUS OF CHARITY GIRLS.

AND

SONG.—"Peerless Phœbe."

No. 4.

WILLIAM is proof against temptation—ARABELLA's despair. | *Enter Phœbe's Schoolfellows, the Charity-girls.*

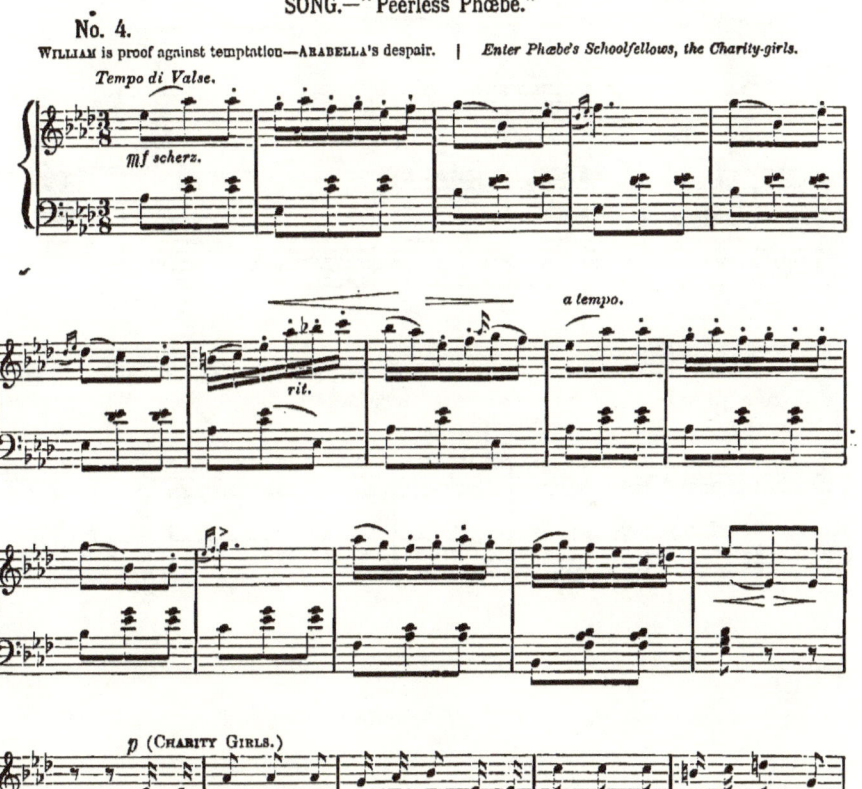

Though we're bred up-on char-i-ty, We have plen-ty hi-lar-i-ty, We

SONG.—PEERLESS PHŒBE.

Of all the girls, the choic-est sam-ple As-sur-ed-ly is Phœ-be, To each one she's a bright ex-am-ple, Who and what-ev-er she be. At

ought to be wed, Or a Squire of high-est de-gree, ... But

she pre-fer'd Wil - li - am Tay-lor in - stead, A sim-ple young

CHARITY GIRLS.
(Giggling.) *mf* SUSAN. *cres.*

gar - den - er he. He, he, A sim - ple young gar - den - er

34

here!   Thanks   for   your   wel - come dear!

SUSAN & GIRLS.

As it

con espressione.
PHŒBE.

Ah!

is   your   wed - ding day,   We   all   of   us   are   gay.

THE TWO RIVERS.

Phœbe and Susan.

No. 5.   SONG.

on her wed-ding day, they say, A girl stands 'twixt two streams of life, One
on the mor-row's tide they float, To cleave for aye their un-known way, And

is the Mai-den yes-ter-day, The oth-er is the mor-row Wife, The
is this bark a sa-fer boat, Than that which bore her yes-ter-day? There

stream that bore her safe be - fore, She leaves, to brave a stran - ger tide, The
may, per - haps, be sad re - gret, There may be joy for ful - filled dreams, But

bark that waits up - on the shore, Is steered by him who calls her "bride." Ye-
nev - er can the wife for - get The day on which she changed the streams. Ye-

38

40

Who will keep the girls in order now? No one. Who will set a good example? No one. Who will win the prizes? No one.

Phœbe's precepts—

" Always seem to be modest and bashful, yet wise,
Remember the value of using your eyes;
Recollect, too, that money's not easily met,
And always accept every offer you get.
Be polite to all—grandmammas, sisters, and mothers,
For they've all of them grandsons, or own sons, or brothers.

And never forget the chief object in life,
Is to quickly be settled—a well-to-do wife."

The wedding gifts of the simple village maiden.— The approach of SIR MINCING LANE and CAPTAIN FLAPPER is signalled by SUSAN—A modest reception—CAPTAIN FLAPPER likes the parish and parishioners—He admires the bride —A contented and grateful peasantry—The simple manners of the country—What PHŒBE FAIRLEIGH may become if WILLIAM follows the example of SIR MINCING LANE, who is essentially

THE SELF-MADE KNIGHT.

Sir Mincing Lane.

No. 6. SONG.

Sir Mincing Lane.

1. Ma-ny years a-go, I made a start With noth-ing, as a gro-cer's boy, I car-ried round par-cels in a light spring cart, And served out pick-les and

2. My mas-ter died, And his wi-dow for-lorn, I sur-vey'd with a kind-ly eye, She was not what is called a beau-ty born, Nor an an-gel from the

3. Of the Ci-ty of Lon-don, Sheriff I was, When we feast-ed the King and court, And his Ma-jes-ty made me a knight, be-cause He es-teem'd our tur-tle and

42

soy,　　　By　dint of　as-sid - u - i - ty, and dex - t'rous hand,　I　rose　a　cash - ier　to
sky;　　When I　told　my　love,　she be-stowed her hand, And her　for - tune my bride to
port.　　I ob - tain'd a　coat　of　arms　of　gor - geous air, And a　first　rate ped - i -

be,　For I　al - ways　mix'd the　su - gar with　sand, And sloe　leaves　sold　for
be,　She was meant, a - las, for a　bet - ter　land, And did - n't live　long　with
gree,　Which　proves that my an - ces-tors　Prin - ces　were, But they had - n't got　L. S.

tea,　For a　self - made man　you　see　in　me,　Not　born of the　a - ris -
me,
D.

made   man   you   see,   is

made   man   you   see,   is

made   man   you   see,   is

44

The Villagers are to eat, drink, and be merry, at SIR MINCINO'S expense. He cannot fail to be popular.
PHŒBE'S soliliquy.—Her determination and strong will expressed in the song.

THE GUILELESS ORPHAN.

No. 7. SONG.   Phœbe.

1. An or-phan, in-no-cent of guile, I am a bash-ful crea-ture; Since
2. When Wil-liam his love dis-closed, My hand in his hand clasp-ing, To

mo-des-ty, the neigh-bors style My most con-spic-uous fea-ture. "Oh!
fy, I felt the most dis-posed, And scarce could speak, for gasp-ing; I

(Curtseys.)

thank you, ma'am!" or, "thank you, sir!" I re - ply to each in the hum - blest tone. What
am not sure what can I say! I mur - mur'd low, in a fal - t'ring tone, "Oh!

ritard.

oth - ers like, I'm sure to pre - fer, With a "please" to him, and a "please" to her.
you must not please go a - way! Well,— if you must,— per - haps I may!"

cres.   *rit.*

Tempo di Valse.

Ah! .... though I an - - swer so, Yet they do not
Ah! .... though I an - - swer'd so, Yet he does not

Tempo di Valse.   *8va*

p

know That I've got a strong will of my own! .... Though I
know That I've got a strong will of my own! .... Though I

8va

cres.

mf

an - swer so, Yet they do not know That I've got a strong will of my
an - swer'd so, Yet he does not know That I've got a strong will of my

colla voce.

Tempo Primo   *1st.*

own!
own!

f   *ritard.*

Allegro.   *2d.*

own!
own!

f Allegro.   *accel.*   *f*

CAPTAIN FLAPPER on the prowl—The abrupt love-making of the Sea-rover—PHŒBE is flattered by the CAPTAIN'S conde-scension—FLAPPER offers to meet the bridegroom in single combat—He salutes the bride, who returns the salute—The mutiny must be suppressed—A respectful scream—Some one comes—Discretion the better part of valor—CRAB to the rescue—His pleadings useless—A blow !—Revenge upon WILLIAM TAYLOR is the idea of CRAB, ARABELLA, and FLAPPER.

REVENGE, REVENGE!

No. 8. TRIO.   Arabella, Capt. Flapper, and Crab.

(Together, in mock tragic style.)

FLAPPER.   ARABELLA.

You will par-don, I am ve-ry sure, the ques-tion, But what is it you in-tend to do? Can

CRAB.   ARA.

no one give us, now, a bright sug-ges-tion? A plan, I think, that I have got, will do! What

ritard. FLAPPER.   CRAB. *p Misterioso.*   (*Whispers to* FLAPPER.)

is it? Speak, I pray! What is it? Pri-thee say!   This is it.

FLAPPER.   CRAB.   (*Whispers to* ARABELLA.)

Oh! de-light-ful! Oh! de-light-ful!   This is it.

52

our revenge we've got. Hush! hush! hush! hush! hush! hush! hush! hush! hush!   hush! hush! hush! hush!   hush!

our revenge we've got. Hush! hush! hush! hush! hush! hush! hush! hush! hush!   hush! hush! hush! hush!   hush!

pp stacc.

hush!   hush!

hush!   hush!

dim.

pp

They go stealthily to work—Hush! Hush! Hush! The happiness of the bride and bridegroom—Their mutual confession—They retire to prepare for their nuptial ceremony. SUSAN announces real man-of-war's men—The crew of His Majesty's ship Thunderbomb, led by the bold bo's'n, BEN BARNACLE—They sing the praises of their vessel.

THE GALLANT THUNDERBOMB.

No. 9. SAILOR'S CHORUS.   **(T. & B.)**

cap - tured full ma - ny a prize, boys! Not a ship in the fleet with

cap - tured full ma - ny a prize, boys! Not a ship in the fleet with

her can com - pete; She can whip a - ny foe twice her size, boys!.... Heave,

her can com - pete; She can whip a - ny foe twice her size, boys! Heave,

cres.

ho!.... Heave, ho! When the big guns blow, When the skulk - ers with af- fright are

ho! Heave, ho! When the big guns blow, When the skulk - ers with af- fright are

weather a-ny sea, If you'll on-ly let her be, There's no craft like the Thun - der -

weather a-ny sea, If you'll on-ly let her be, There's no craft like the Thun - der -

- bomb, Thunderbomb, boys!

- bomb, Thunderbomb, Thunderbomb, boys!

ALL ON ACCOUNT OF ELIZA.

No. 10. ROMANCE.   Ben Barnacle.

BARNACLE'S inquiries— SUSAN'S question, " What brought you here, Eliza ?"

1. The yarn as I am a-bout to spin, Is all on account of E - li - za, I'll
2. I've nearly been blown a - way in a gale, All on account of E - li - za, And I've

tell you how I was ta-ken in, All on account of E - li - za; She
al-most been eat - en up by a whale, All on account of E - li - za; I've had

said that she'd ev-er be   true to one, But she bolted a-way with a son of a gun! So I
sword cuts by dozens, And I've been shot thro' I've   had yellow fe-ver, and al-so the blue; I've been

CHORUS.
SOPR.

All   on account,   all   on account,   all   on account of E - li - za,

TENOR.

All   on account,   all   on account,   all   on account of E - li - za,

BASS.

He   cut   his   stick, and to sea he   run;   All   on account of E - li - za.
He's been bitten by   sharks, and by crocodiles, too;

He   cut   his   stick, and to sea he   run;   All   on account of E - li - za.
He's been bitten by   sharks, and by crocodiles, too;

3. My du-ty is now, smart lads to press; All on account of E - li - za, If
4. I've courted the la - dies, all thro' my life; All on account of E - li - za, But

they say "No!" why I say "Yes!" All on account of E - li - za; So
never could steer to the pro - per wife; All on account of E - li - za; I've

rit.   *a tempo.*

look up, my mess-mates, some boys for the sea, And if to your summons they do not a - gree, Why,
kiss'd, and I've hugg'd them in ev' - ry port, The fat and the lean, the tall and the short, But,

WEDDING CHORUS.

No. 11.

(S, S, T, & B.)

62

Ding a ding dong ding a ding, ding dong ding dong ding dong ding, ding dong ding dong ding dong ding dong ding.

Ding dong ding a dong, ding dong ding dong ding dong ding, ding dong ding dong ding dong ding dong ding.

Ding dong ding dong ding dong ding ding, ding dong

f Lento.

Marcato.

p

(Enter Pressgang.)
Misterioso.

pp

tr

FINALE.

No. 12.

The arrest of WILLIAM TAYLOR !—BARNACLE is sympathetic, but unyielding to all entreaties—CRAB, the man of peace, is also bound for a man-of-war.

BILLEE.

BEN BARNACLE.

'Tis hard by fate thus to be part - ed. Cheer up, messmate I don't be dow

- heart - ed, For I, like you, leave love and beau - ty, A - board our craft to do my

du - ty. Fall in! close up! we must a - way! we must a - way!

66

far you range, My love for you shall ne-ver, ne-ver, ne-ver, ne-ver, ne-ver change.

far you range, Her love for you shall ne-ver, ne-ver, ne-ver, ne-ver, ne-ver change.

far you range, Her love for you shall ne-ver, ne-ver, ne-ver, ne-ver, ne-ver change.

Allegretto.   *p* BILLEE.

Shoul

PHŒBE.   BILLEE.

I come back with-out o - ver a leg, Still I'll be true to you;........ Should I

stump a - bout on a wood - en peg, Still I'll be true to you...... Should I

be be - reft of the sight of my eyes, Should cuts on my arms have re - duced their size, Should I

ritard.　　　　　　　　　　　　PHŒBE.

come back to you with a par - cel of lies; Still I'll be true to you......

colla voce.　　　　　　　　*p*

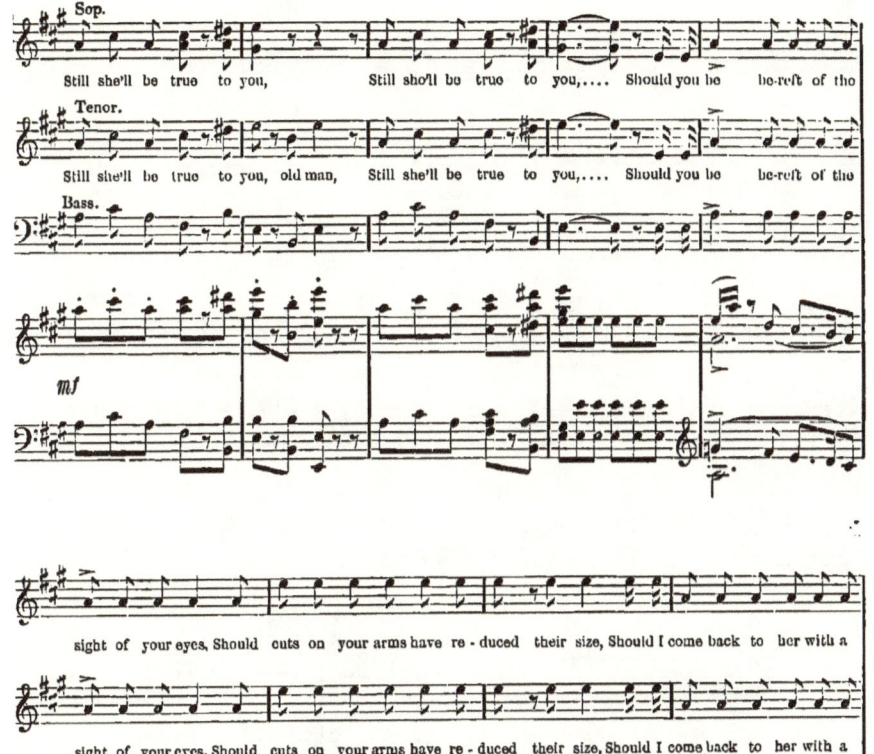

Sop.
Still she'll be true to you, Still she'll be true to you,.... Should you be be-reft of the

Tenor.
Still she'll be true to you, old man, Still she'll be true to you,.... Should you be be-reft of the

Bass.

mf

sight of your eyes, Should cuts on your arms have re - duced their size, Should I come back to her with a

sight of your eyes, Should cuts on your arms have re - duced their size, Should I come back to her with a

(Enter Sir Mincing Lane, Arabella and Captain Flapper.)

par - cel of lies, Still she'll be true to you.

par - cel of lies, Still she'll be true to you.

SIR MINCING.   FLAPPER.

Come, what's all this?   His war - rant see!

ARABELLA. *(Imploringly.)*

O fa - ther, fa - ther, save him,

brave boys, off, for the loug boat waits, And we must cruise upon the brine, oh, But we'll soon come back on

Tenor.

brave boys, off, for the long boat waits, And we must cruise upon the brine, oh, But we'll soon come back on

Bass.

f

home - ward tack, With our pock - ets full of rhi - no, With a fav - 'ring gale we

home - ward tack, With our pock - ets full of rhi - no, With a fav - 'ring gale we

shall set sail, When the canvas taut will swell, oh, So here's a parting glass, and a kiss for ev-'ry lass, And to

shall set sail, When the canvas taut will swell, oh, So here's a parting glass, and a kiss for ev-'ry lass, And to

ev - 'ry one a long fare - well, a long fare - well, oh! With a fav - 'ring gale we

Sop. _ff_ (*Principals also.*)

Tenor.

ev - 'ry one a long fare - well, a long fare - well, oh! With a fav - 'ring gale we

Bass.

kiss for ev - 'ry lass, And to ev - 'ry one a long fare - well, a long fare -

kiss for ev - 'ry lass, And to ev - 'ry one a long fare - well, a long fare -

- well, oh! A - way, a - way, a - way, a - way, a - way, a - way, a -

- well, oh! Fare - well, fare - well, Fare - well, fare - well, fare

- well, oh! Hoo - ray! hoo - ray! hoo - ray! hoo - ray! hoo - ray! hoo - ray! hoo

- well, oh! A - way, a - way, a - way, a - way, a - way, a - way, a -

- way, a - way, a - way, a - way, a - way, a - way, a -

- well,..................... fare - well,..................... fare -

- ray! hoo - ray! hoo - ray! hoo - ray! hoo - ray! hoo - ray! h

- way,.......... A - way,.......... a - - way!

- well,.......... Fare - well,.......... fare - - well!

- ray!.......... Hoo - ray!.......... hoo - ray!

- way,.......... A - way,.......... a - - way!

Grandioso.

cres.

ƒ

ƒƒ

ACT II :

BACK AGAIN.

No. 13.　OPENING CHORUS.　(S. S. T. B.)

SCENE—*At Portsmouth—The harbour in the distance.*

Van-quish-ers of France and Spain, Ru-lers of the sea. Far they roam, far they roam Wel-com

Van-quish-ers of France and Spain, Ru-lers of the sea. Far they roam, far they roam Wel-com

home, welcome home, welcome home, wel - come home...........

home, welcome home, welcome, wel - come home...........

home, welcome home, welcome home, wel - come home...........

BALLET MUSIC.

INTRODUCTION.

82

BLACK COOK'S DANCE.

84

THE POOR, WICKED MAN.

No. 14. SONG.   (Crab.)

The Terpsichorean revels natural to the British tar. CRAB, *the mariner—his profession changes but his character the same—No villainy to do.*
Allegro Moderato.

1. I'm a vil-lain of the deep-est dye, Or rath-er I should like to
2. When a ped-a-gogue, I'd oft-en wish, To give priz-es to the worst at

be, No mat-ter tho' how hard I try, I nev-er get an op-por-tu-ni-
school, The good boys I would long to swish, But I could not car-ry out the

.tee. So my life re-sembles taste-less salt, Or gin-ger-bread that has no spice. But
rule. To scut-tle ships I'd like to try, A trait-or's game I think is nice. Such

vice.   For I'm such an un‿for‿tu‿nate vil‿lain,   A Bor‿gi‿a born out of

Allegretto.

time.... Is there nev‿er a plan for a poor wick‿ed man, To ac‿com‿plish some ter‿ri‿ble

crime........ I'm such an un‿for‿tu‿nate vil‿lain,   A Bor‿gi‿a born out of

time...... Is there nev-er a plan, for a poor wick-ed man To ac-com-plish some ter-ri-ble

crime! ter-ri-ble crime!

tempo 1o.

88

Meditating on crime—Eliza Dabsey on the lookout for Ben Barnacle—The recognition—The news of Phœbe's flight—Who was the "he?"—The danger of life on a cutter—The Parthian warfarer. William and Arabella—Familiarity does not always breed contempt. The emotion caused by a sail on the ocean expressed in—

THE BALLAD OF THE BILLOW.
(Arabella and Billee.)

No. 15. SONG.

Andante con espressione. ARABELLA.

1. When I was a-float in the cock-le boat, And you were be-side me, dear, I had ne-ver a qualm, Tho' I longed for a calm, For I felt,—I must own it—queer, When you pressed my hand, How I wished for land, Yet I

2. When the wind fierce blew I crept near to you, As we sped o'er the an-gry sea; When the gale grew worse, You were still my nurse, And you tend-ed me care-ful-lee, Yes I must con-fess, That no stew-ard-ess Could have

be with me still, To pro - tect and to suc-cor your wife.....................

rain, snow, or hail, You shall soothe my mis - giv-ings a - now.....................

ARABELLA. *Tempo di Valse.*

MAJORE.

O my darling! when winds blow foul, when there's groaning and moaning a - baft............ On

BILLEE.

O my dar - ling! when there's groaning and moaning a - baft.... .... On

Tempo di Valse.

mf MAJORE.

windward or lee-ward, My skip-per and stew-ard, The cap-tain and crew of our craft.

THE FAITHFUL CREW.

No. 16. (Phœbe and Chorus.)

ARABELLA promises that SIR MINCING LANE will "come down" handsomely—How BILLER obtained his promotion—
The advantage of a runaway horse—*Veni, vidi, vici!*—The man sacrificed to the weak mortal—The loss of fourpence,
or, rather, of a damning piece of evidence—PHŒBE and the Runaways.

Voice.

Allegretto.

f PHŒBE. GIRLS. (*off.*)

Hi! hallo! Hi! hallo!

Piano.

f

PHŒBE. GIRLS. (*off.*) *f* PHŒBE. *ad lib.*

Hi! hallo! Hi! hallo! hal - lo! ....

cres - cen - do.

PHŒBE.
I followed my darling Bill to sea, We all of us followed you. I

GIRLS.

PHŒBE.

GIRLS.

PHŒBE.
followed him to a far countree. We all of us followed too; But though

dangers we've seen, And tho' ship-wreck'd we've been, We have never yet found Bil - lee; He's been

GIRLS.

fighting the foe, But we all of us know, He will come back a - gain from sea. He will

PHŒBE.

come back a - gain from sea to you. And his heart, well I know, is ev - er true, And his

PHŒBE.

heart, well I know, is ev - er true!

So

mf GIRLS.

To you, to you, to you, to you! He has

true! . . . . And his heart, well I know, is ev - er true! His

come back a - gain, from sea to you, to you! . . . . His

heart, I know, is ev - er true, Well, I know, is ev - er true!

heart, to you, will e'er be true, Will ev - er be true to you!

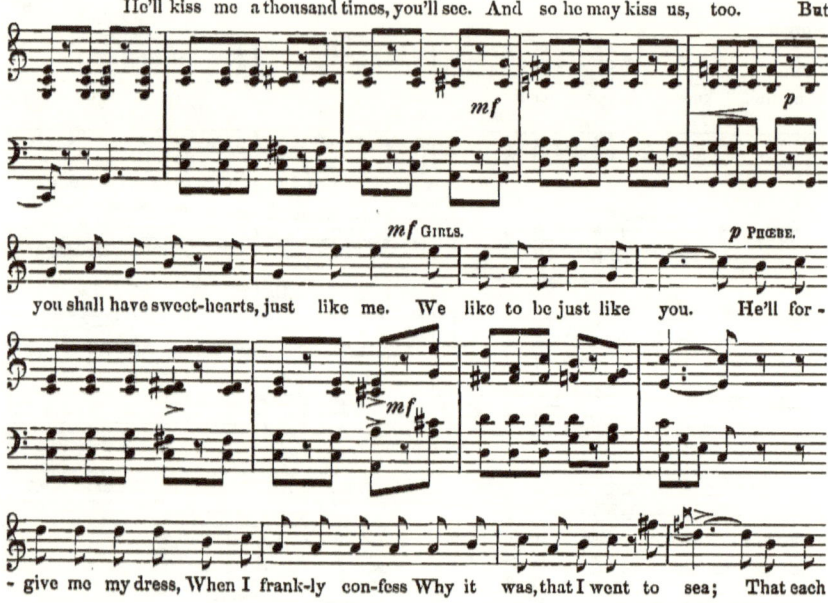

He'll kiss me a thousand times, you'll see. And so he may kiss us, too. But you shall have sweet-hearts, just like me. We like to be just like you. He'll for- give me my dress, When I frank-ly con-fess Why it was, that I went to sea; That each

float to find your Bil-lee for you. While his heart, well I know, is ev-er true, While his

heart, well I know, is ev-er true!

mf GIRLS.

To you, to you, to you, to you! Went a-

So

true! . . . . While his heart, well I know, is ev-er true! His

heart, I know, is ev - er true, Well, I know, is ev - er true!

heart, to you will e'er be true, Will ev- er be true to you,

cres - cen - do.

Will be ev - er true, Will

you, Will be ev - er true to you, to you!

IN DAYS GONE BY.

No. 16. DUET AND CHORUS. (Billee, Phœbe, and Chorus.)

The letter not found. Phœbe not recognised. Want of politeness. A session in manners

BILLEE. 1. In days gone by our sires would try To be to all po-
PHŒBE. 2. In mod-ern days our mod-ern ways, Have lost the grand old

-lite......... To friend or foe they'd al-ways show Such manners ex-qui-site......(PHŒBE) No
style......... For in the street the friends we meet Give nod, or wink, or smile......(BILLEE)But

sign could tell folks half so well, The true Ar-is-to-crat, As smiling face and court-ly grace Of
still you see there rules must be, For those who'd shirk the cat; With heels well clos'd, and fi-gure posed, You

gal - lants had to do was— just like that. Just like that,
sai - lors have to do is— just like that. Just like that,

Just like that, Noth - ing but a move - ment with a hat; You
Just like that, Fin - gers brought up smart - ly to the hat; You

do the thing po - lite-ly, You smile, and sim-per brightly, All that gallants had to do was—
make the movement slightly, You touch the brim quite light-ly, All that sai - lors had to do was—

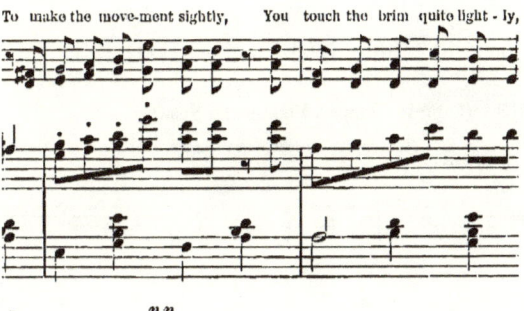

To make the move-ment sightly,   You touch the brim quite light - ly,

pp

TRIM LITTLE PHŒBE.

No. 17. TRIO. (Captain Flapper, Phœbe and Susan.)

A cold welcome—How to act. FLAPPER, *the Lovelace, follows* SUSAN—*The Voice of Conscience—* "RICHARD CARR" *Never repulsed—Yes, once by* PHŒBE.

1. A trim lit-tle craft was Phœ - be, Was Phœ - be, was Phœ - be, A slim lit-tle earth - ly He - be, Yes, He - be, Yes, He - be, She re
2. Her lov - er was Bil - lee Tay - lor, Was Tay - lor, was Tay - lor, He left her to be a sai - lor, A sai - lor, a sai - lor, But

PHŒBE. *(sneeringly.)* *(2d anxiously.)*   FLAPPER.   SUSAN. *(laughingly.)* *(2d v.anxiously.)*   FLAPPER.

pelled me,'twas sad! She repelled him,how sad! But her charms drove me mad, But her charms drove him mad, But I
in the Na - vee, But in the Na - vee He's found there may be, He's found there may be As good

mf   *p*   *p colla.*

ritard.   PHŒBE & SUSAN. FLAPPER.   *ad lib.* (Spoken.) *tempo.*   *rit.*   *tempo.*

loved her,'fore gad. But you see!— Well! She would not hear............ me........ Per -
fish in the sea! Not at all— Well! Not at all dear - - er.......... Per -

voce.   *cres.*   *dolce*

PHŒBE & SUSAN.   *p*   *cres.*

- haps it was wrong,but I loved her, How long He loved her how long?............
- haps it was wrong,for he loved her, How long He loved her how long?............

FLAPPER.

I lov - ed her............ Per -
He lov - ed her............ But per

cres.

How long? You loved her how long.........
How long? He loved her how

haps it was wrong But I loved her, I lov - ed her her......... Well as
haps it was wrong for he loved her, he loved her

cres. *ritard.* *cres.*

long as the darling was near me. 2. Her

mf *p*

long......... Well as long as the vil- lain was near her But nev-er-the-less I still must confess A

FLAPPER *relates the love adventures of* LIEUTENANT WILLIAM TAYLOR—*Never be inconstant*—MRS. DABSEY—*A Prize!*
a Sail! the Chase! SIR MINCING LANE's *Volunteers!—An Idea.*

WITH FIFE AND DRUM.

No. 18.   CHORUS OF VOLUNTEERS.   (S. S. T. B.)

(*Enter* SIR MINCING LANE *and Volunteers.*)

er, From Eng-land's shore, now, as of yore, We'll

er, From Eng-land's shore, now, as of yore, We'll

da. Our foe-men hear, with rage and fear, That

da. Our foe-men hear, with rage and fear, That

ble, For the loy - al cheers of the Vol - un - teers Make

(TENORI & BASSI *only*.)

(them) *p stacc.*

in the least ap-palls us, So here we are a gal-lant, gal-lant band, To

p stacc.

in the least ap-palls us, So here we are a gal-lant, gal-lant band, To

(SOPRANI *also*.)

f

do or die for old Eng-land, for old Eng - land . . .

f

do or die for old Eng-land, for old Eng - land . . .

f

Moderato.

Sir MINCING LANE.

p

See, the gro-cer is callous of his figs.

See the

Scherz.

p

p

Tempo Io.
(Sir MINCING *also.*)

reg - u - lars   are   all   ve - ry   well,   The   in - fant - ry   or

reg - u - lars   are   all   ve - ry   well,   The   in - fant - ry   or

Tempo Io.

gren - a - diers,   But to stand up - on   the strand,   And to guard their na - tive land,   Who so

gren - a - diers,   But to stand up - on   the strand,   And to guard their na - tive land,   Who so

brave   as   the   Vol - un - teers!   Who   so   brave   as   the   Vol - un-

brave   as   the   Vol - un - teers!   Who   so   brave   as   the   Vol - un-

die   for   old   Eng - land,   for   old   Eng

die   for   old   Eng - land,   for   old   Eng   -   -

114

CONCERTED PIECE AND SONG.

Ben Barnacle, Sir Mincing Lane,
No. 19.
Phœbe, Flapper, and Chorus.
(S. S. T. B.)

SIR MINCING.

ours! his coat will soon be red, On shore hence-forth he'll fight, in - stead, And from the sea will

se - ver, For e - ver! For ev - er! Look here, we ain't a

SOPRANOS.
For ev - er! For ev - er!

TENORS.
For ev - er! For ev - er!

BASSES.
For ev - er! For ev - er!

going to lose, The smart-est lad of all our crews; He'll fight a - mong the old true blues, Or

116

FLAPPER. *recit.*

Stop, stop! nor mo-ral laws des-pise, By blacking thus each other's eyes.

Brave messmates bear with him, For I can tell the rea-son why. Let's hear, let's hear the reason why!

SIR MINCING.

Let's hear, let's hear the reason why!

Let's hear, let's hear the reason why!

Let's hear, let's hear the reason why!

SONG. "LOVE, LOVE, LOVE."

No. 19. a.

1. Do you know why the rabbits are caught in the snares, Or the tab-by cats shot in the tiles? Why the ti-gers and li-ons creep out of their lairs, Why an os-trich will travel for miles? Do you know why a sane man will whimper or cry, And

2. Do you know why a plain girl will think her-self fair? Or a clever man wisdom re-fuse? Do you know why a dwarf ris-es yards in the air, And a gi-ant sinks in-to his shoes? Do you know why a brave man takes refuge in flight While a

weep o'er a rib-bon or glove? . . . Why a cook will put su-gar for salt in a pie, Do you
cow-ard no dan-ger can move? Why night be-comes day, and why day be-comes night, Do you

know? . . . . . Well, I'll tell you, it's love, . . it's love. . .

Love! love! love! The first born of cre - a - tion! Love! love! love! the god of ev -'ry na - tion!

Love, love, love in each and ev' - ry sta - tion, The ru - ler of the u - ni - verse is Love! love!

Love, love, love in each and ev' - ry sta - tion, The ru - ler of the u - ni - verse is Love! love!

Love, love, love in each and ev' - ry sta - tion, The ru - ler of the u - ni - verse is Love! love!

rall.

love!

love!

love!

ff Presto.

The power of Love exemplified —BARNACLE's suggestion —The usual thing — ELIZA again! FLAPPER gives chase, as does BENJAMIN —
The position of son-in-law to a rich knight not to be despised, in WILLIAM's estimation — The gross familiarity of CRAB receives an
unpleasant check — CRAB cries for vengeance.
BARNACLE cuts out the CAPTAIN and brings in ELIZA a prize — FLAPPER follows with sword and pistol — His own bo'sum! not one of
Mother Carey's chicken's either — Disgust of FLAPPER — BARNACLE takes possession of the weapons — The lass that loves a sailor.
PHŒBE's fruitless search.
A tar in tears — Mutual recognition —WILLIAM's marraige announced — PHŒBE's despair, rage, and resolution! Revenge!

CONCERTED PIECE.

No. 20.   PHŒBE, BARNACLE, AND SAILORS.

(T. B.)

See here, my lads, what would you do, If you should find your love un-true, And court- ing with a-

Just tell you what we would do, And save a deal of bo - ther!

(forcibly.)

We'd ei - ther punch that o - ther's head, Or fix him with an

Tremoloso.

f *rall.*

ounce of lead, And shoot the ras - cal dead, dead, dead. That's what we'd do,

That's what we'd do, that's what we'd do, that's what we'd do! I

That's what we'd do, that's what we'd do, that's what we'd do!

That's what we'd do, that's what we'd do, that's what, that's what we'd do!

al - most, al - - most dare — I will, I will pre -

pare! . . . So quick-ly bring me sword and pis - tol, Forth to come at

127

128

On the track of the deceiver!
WILLIAM and ARABELLA name the happy day—CRAB the Spy! CRAB's look-out—Ho, ho! delectable villany!
The lovers! the start! the catastrophe—Arrest of RICHARD CARR.

(A) CONCERTED PIECE. "I AM NO MAN."

No. 21. PHŒBE, ARABELLA, BILLEE, FLAPPER & CHORUS. S. S. T. B.

(B) Quarrelling Duet. PHŒBE and ARABELLA.

PHŒBE.
p dolce.

Yes, yes, I am a wo - man!

FLAPPER.

Ex - plain this mar - vel - lous as -

p dolce.

FLAPPER.   PRINCIPALS ALSO.

ritard.
PHŒBE.

ser - tion! Ex- plain! ex - plain!   ex - plain! ex - plain!   'Tis not be-

Ex- plain! ex - plain!   ex - plain! ex - plain!

Ex- plain! ex - plain!   ex - plain! ex - plain!

CHORUS

PHŒBE

cause of your co - er - cion,   But I'll ex - plain, I will ex - plain.

He will ex - plain.

She will ex - plain.

Allegro vivace.

QUARRELLING DUET.

PHŒBE.
ARABELLA.

(Phœbe.) 1. Not ve - ry long a - go, I loved So
(Arabella.) 2. Not ve - ry long a - go, I loved,My

tru - ly that I thought, My heart could nev - er be un-moved, And his could ne'er be bought. Our
heart was not my own, And still to day it is un-moved, And he has kind - er grown. Of

rall - en - - tan -

wedding day had dawn'd so gay, The bells rang out for me, When four and twen - ty sea - men came And
vil-lage maid I'm not a - fraid,Tho' dress'd in tra - ves - tie; For Bil - lee Tay - lor is my own, And

rall - en - cres. tan -

- do. (to Billee.) tempo. p mf

press'd him for the sea. For I'm Phœbe, Phœ-be, Phœbe, Yes I am, you sneak, I am Phœbe, Phœbe,
thinks a - lone for me. For I'm A - ra, A - ra-bel - la, Not a-bash'd you see; I am A - ra, A - ra-

PHŒBE.   accel.

Phœbe, Whom you thought ve - ry weak,   I am Phœ - be, Phœ - be, Phœ - be,   Dare you look or speak,   If
bel-la, Who'll be wed-ded   to   Bil - lee,   I am A - ra,   A - ra - bel - la, Who sent him off to sea,   And I

SOPRANOS.
(Principals also.)

She is Phœ - be, Phœ - be, Phœ - be,   Dare you look or speak,   If
She is A - ra,   A - ra - bel - la, Who sent him off to sea,   And

TENORS.

She is Phœ - be, Phœ - be, Phœ - be,   Dare you look or speak,   If
She is A - ra,   A - ra - bel - la, Who sent him off to sea,   And she

BASSES.

She is Phœ - be, Phœ - be, Phœ - be,   Dare you look or speak,   If
She is A - ra,   A - ra - bel - la, Who sent him off to sea,   And she

cres.   f accell.

Tempo 1o.
ARABELLA.

so, then you'll not find your Phœbe weak! weak! weak! 2. Not weak!
mean to keep him, all of him, for me! me! me!

so, then you'll not find your Phœbe weak! weak! weak!   weak!
means to keep him, all of him, does she! she! she!   she!

so, then you'll not find your Phœbe weak! weak! weak!   weak!
means to keep him, all of him, does she! she! she!   she!

so, then you'll not find your Phœbe weak! weak! weak!   weak!
means to keep him, all of him, does she! she! she!   she!

cres.   cres.

The rescue of CRAB! The witness from the sea—The French Commander's letter! Can BILLEE TAYLOR be a coward?

GRAND FINALE.

BILLER

vir - tu - ous cow - ard, let me be, let me be, let me be, A

Let him be, let him be A

Let him be, let him be, A

Let him be, let him be, A

FLAPPER

vir - tu - ous cow-ard, let me be. Sure such re-marks should

vir - tu - ous cow-ard, let him be.

vir - tu - ous cow -ard, let him be.

vir - tu - ous cow-ard, let him be.

scherz.

135

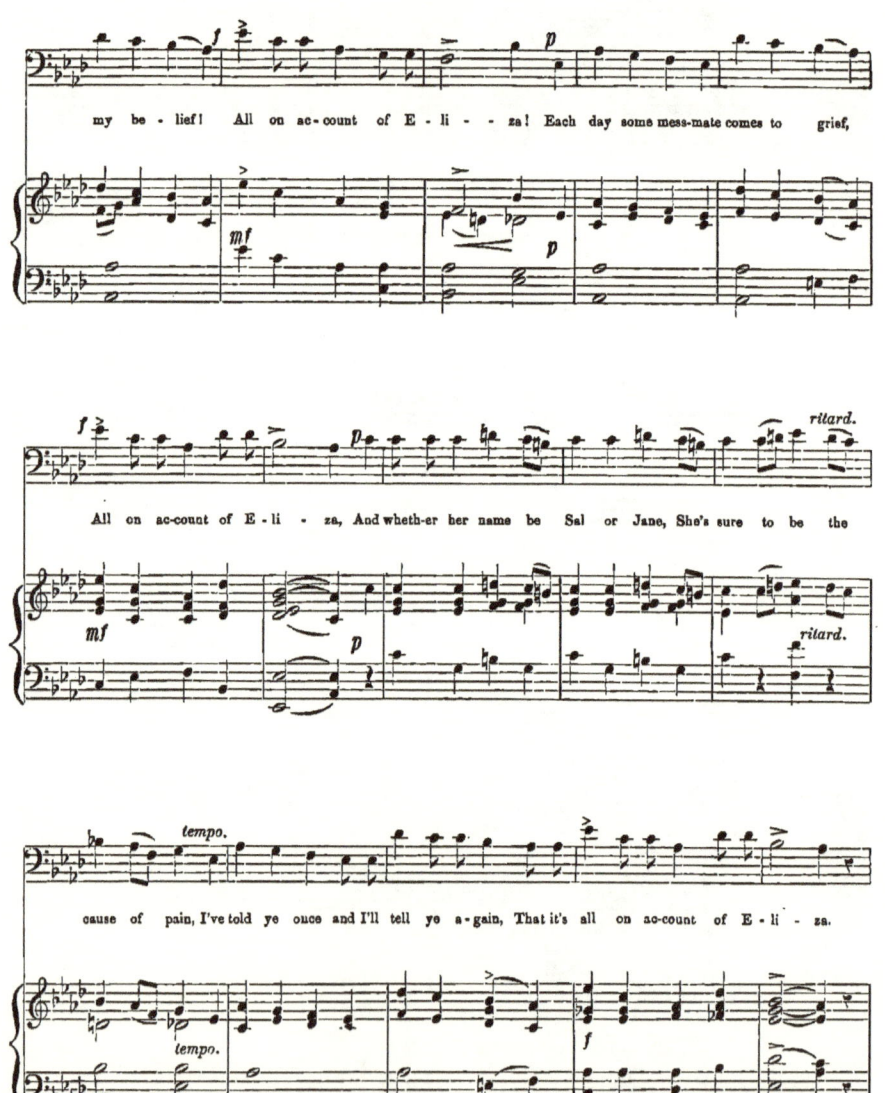

my be - lief! All on ac - count of E - li - - za! Each day some mess-mate comes to grief,

All on ac-count of E - li - za, And wheth-er her name be Sal or Jane, She's sure to be the

cause of pain, I've told ye once and I'll tell ye a - gain, That it's all on ac-count of E - li - za.

Love! love! love! the first born of cre-a-tion

Love! love! love! the first born of cre-tion

Love! love! love! the first born of cre-a-tion

Con Spirito.

Love! love! love! the god of ev'-ry na-tion, Love! love! love! in

Love! love! love! the god of ev'-ry na-tion, Love! love! love! in

Love! love! love! the god of ev'-ry na-tion, Love! love! love! in

each and ev-'ry sta-tion, The ru-ler of the u - ni-verse is Love! love! love!............

each and ev-'ry sta-tion, The ru-ler of the u - ni-verse, is Love! love! love!............

www.ingramcontent.com/pod-product-compliance
Lightning Source LLC
Chambersburg PA
CBHW020235030726
47497CB00009B/3112